The Missing Story Mystery

Dalmatian Press, LLC, 2008. All rights reserved. Printed in the U.S.A.
The DALMATIAN PRESS name and logo are trademarks of Dalmatian Publishing Group, LLC, Franklin, Tennessee 37067. 1-866-418-2572.
No part of this book may be reproduced or copied in any form without written permission from the copyright owner.

08 09 10   NGS 10 9 8 7 6 5 4 3 2 1
16335 Disney My Friends Tigger & Pooh 8x8 - The Missing Story Mystery

One day, in the Hundred-Acre Wood, a siren was sounded, calling the…

SSuuuUUpppperrr ssIIIEEEUUtthhs!

Tigger and Pooh and Darby and Buster gathered at the Changing Tree, ready to solve a mystery—because that's what Super Sleuths do best!

"Time to slap my cap!" said Darby. "Let's see what the Finder Flag shows us."

"Look!" said Pooh.

"A book—and Roo!" said Tigger.

"Maybe Roo is reading a mystery book," suggested Pooh.

"Dunno," said Tigger, "but ol' Roo-Boy *is* trying to 'page' us—hoo-hoo-hoo!"

"Come on, Super Sleuths! Let's say the oath!" called Darby.

"Any time, any place,
The Super Sleuths are on the case!"

The Super Sleuths found a very droopy Roo outside his house.
"What's wrong, Roo?" asked Darby.

"I can't find my storybook," said Roo quietly. "Mama has been reading it to me. I like it so much that I took it with me this morning when I went outside. But now I can't find it—and—and—and I will never know how the story ends."

"Hmmm…" said Tigger. "A reg-a-lar missing story mystery."

"Don't worry, Roo. We'll solve this mystery," said Darby.
"First we have to start asking questions."
"Okay," said Tigger. "What's 19 + 6?"

"Not that kind of question," said Darby. "Think, think, think, Roo. Where have you been today?"

"Well, I went to Rabbit's house this morning," said Roo.

"Then, let's go over to Rabbit's house. Come on!" said Darby.

"What is the story about?" asked Piglet as they walked over to Rabbit's house.

"Oh!" sighed Roo. "It is a wonderful story! You see, once upon a time there was a hummingbird…"

"A humming bird," said Pooh. "I like hums—and humming."

"…and the hummingbird flitted about the garden all day. She loved the flowers, but she was a little lonely. Flowers don't talk, you know. Then, one day, she met a big green caterpillar—and they became friends!"

Roo interrupted his story to search around Rabbit's garden. The friends looked and looked—but they could not find Roo's storybook.

"To solve this mystery, you'll need to retrace your steps, Roo," said Darby. "Where did you go next?"

"Pooh Sticks Bridge," said Roo.

"Let's scooter-oo to the bridge of the sticks of Pooh!" said Tigger.

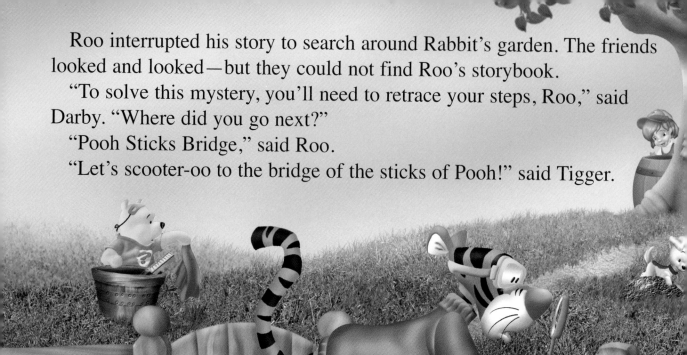

Piglet whispered to Roo, "I like your story, Roo. It's such a happy story."

"Yes, but it does get sad…" said Roo.

"Sad? Tell some more, please," said Eeyore.

"Well, this part is still happy," said Roo. "The hummingbird and the caterpillar played every morning in the big garden. They played hide-and-seek. They sang songs. And they would sit on a flower together and find shapes in the clouds."

"Were there, by chance, any bees in the garden? Honeybees?" asked Pooh hopefully.

"No bees," said Roo.

And when they got to Pooh Sticks Bridge...

...no book.

"Super Sleuths don't give up!" announced Tigger. "Where did you go next, Roo-Boy?"

Roo sighed. "I don't remember… I'll never know how the story ends…"

"Seems to me that the hummingbird and the caterpillar just live happily ever after," offered Pooh.

Roo sighed again. "I'm afraid not. You see…

…one morning, the caterpillar told the hummingbird that he had no time to play. The hummingbird watched as his friend made a brown case all around himself. 'Why is he making that?' thought the hummingbird.

"He waited and waited for the caterpillar to come out. But the caterpillar never did.

"The hummingbird came the next day, and the next day, and the next day. He called and called, but his friend did not come and play."

"That *is* kinda sad," said Eeyore, "if I do say so myself."

Roo looked up at his friends.

"The hummingbird was all alone in the garden…" he said.

Suddenly Roo leaped up.

"The garden!" he cried. "That's where I went next!"

"But… we went to Rabbit's vegetable garden," said Darby.

"No—the flower garden in the big meadow! I went to look for caterpillars!" said Roo.

"Then, let's all go to the garden in the meadow!" said Darby. "Everybody up for some more sleuthing?"

"Yep-a-roo!" said Tigger. "Mystery loves company!"

All the sleuthers marched merrily off to the garden.

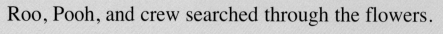

Roo, Pooh, and crew searched through the flowers.

And there, right next to some daisies, was Roo's storybook!

"My book!" squealed Roo. "My storybook!"

"It was right where you forgot to remember it!" said Piglet.

"Thank you, everyone, for helping me find my book," said Roo.

"Still a sad story, though," said Eeyore glumly. "Don't know how it ends."

"Let's go ask your mama to finish reading the story, Roo," said Darby.

"Yes, yes, yes!" cried Roo.

Kanga was very happy to finish the story.
"Not too long after, a wonderful thing happened.
The hummingbird was sipping nectar from a flower—
when he heard a familiar voice: 'Hello, friend!
It's me! How do I look?'

"The hummingbird turned around—and saw a beautiful butterfly! 'I've changed!' said the caterpillar. 'Now I can fly and play with you—every day!'

"You see," said Kanga, "a caterpillar does not stay a caterpillar. It builds itself a case called a chrysalis. It stays inside the chrysalis for about two weeks—and changes—and comes out as a butterfly!"

"Yay!" cheered Roo. "I'm so glad we know the ending!"

"I think," said Pooh, "that the hummingbird and the butterfly played Butterfly Tag all spring...

...and they lived flappily ever after!"

24029 6023